D0845420

GORF

Gorf in the guise of a woman.

ALSO BY MICHAEL McCLURE

The Adept
The Beard
Dark Brown
Gargoyle Cartoons
Ghost Tantras
Hymns to St. Geryon
Jaguar Skies
Little Odes
The Mad Cub
Meat Science Essays
The New Book / A Book of Torture
Passage
Rare Angel
September Blackberries
Star

GORF

or GORF AND THE BLIND DYKE

Michael McClure

A NEW DIRECTIONS BOOK

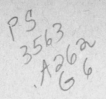

Copyright © 1974, 1976 by Michael McClure
Copyright © 1976 by the Magic Theater

All rights reserved. Except for brief passages quoted in a newspaper, magazine, radio, or television review, no part of this book may be reproduced in any form or by any means, electronic or mechanical, including photocopying and recording, or by any information storage and retrieval system, without permission in writing from the Publisher.

Gorf was first published in its entirety in *The CoEvolution Quarterly* (Summer 1974), to whose editors grateful acknowledgment is made.

Caution: Professionals and amateurs are hereby warned that *Gorf,* being fully protected under the copyright laws of the United States of America, the British Empire including the Dominion of, Canada, and all other countries of the Copyright Union, is subject to royalty. All rights, including professional, amateur, motion picture, recitation, lecturing, public reading, radio and television broadcasting, and the rights of translation into foreign languages, are strictly reserved. Particular emphasis is laid on the question of readings, permission for which must be secured from the author's agent, Claire S. Degener, c/o The Sterling Lord Agency, 660 Madison Avenue, New York 10021.

Manufactured in the United States of America
First published clothbound and as New Directions Paperbook 416 in 1976
Published simultaneously in Canada by McClelland & Stewart, Ltd.

Library of Congress Cataloging in Publication Data

McClure, Michael.
  Gorf: or, Gorf and the blind dyke (The purple hero cycle)

  (A New Directions Book)
  I. Title. II. Title: The purple hero cycle.
PS3563.A262G6   812'.5'4   76–14932
ISBN 0–8112–0630–0
ISBN 0–8112–0612–2 pbk.

New Directions Books are published for James Laughlin
by New Directions Publishing Corporation,
333 Sixth Avenue, New York 10014

This play is dedicated to John Lion

INTRODUCTION

Man's capacity for renewal and rebirth is tied to his ability to remain in touch with his child self. From here he can re-experience his sense of animal optimism, his ability to transform at will, his pleasure in free floating as well as free falling. This is the consciousness from which Michael Mc-Clure has written *Gorf* and from which I directed it. I don't want to imply that there is anything esoteric about *Gorf*—followers of McClure's theater will find the same wild humor and consciousness of American forms that were displayed in his earlier *Gargoyle Cartoons,* but with new dimensions of plot and characterization.

Michael McClure's *Gorf* is a comic-heroic return of drama to its origins in the epic mysteries. A child *circa* 600 B.C. living in Greece was probably as much in awe of the image of the winged phallus as a modern day child who confronts the Goodyear blimp. Both are miraculous. They are symbols of colossal expansiveness and glimpses of the benign, smiling side of the unknown.

Take a flying cock and balls, a blind motorcycle Lesbian, a pair of dancing TV sets, a hard-hat laborer and his wife, shepherds, motorcycle outlaws, naked tap-dancing stars, a fairy girl, and a giant hairy elephant's hindquarters. Accompany them with sounds issuing from a band of cherubs playing a range of styles from Puccini to Spike Jones—and throw them into a plot that echoes everything from *Oedipus at*

Colonus to *Who's Afraid of Virginia Woolf?* You still haven't exhausted *Gorf*'s parameters. It is a party in eternity, a bubble.

There are moments in life that are visionary—Shelley's sight of Mount Blanc, and Carl Sagan's inveighing against "liquid chauvinism" at the conference on Communication with Extraterrestrial Intelligence. Such moments are ahistorical, oceanic, a momentary waking from the dream of history, a dancing toward Bethlehem to be reborn. *Gorf* is a fox trot toward the Shitfer by way of the Bump.

JOHN LION

The first production of *Gorf* was directed by John Lion and produced in February 1974 by the Magic Theater at The Firehouse in San Francisco. The music director was Daniel Orsborn, with choreography by Patrese Lovecraft, sound by Dan Dugan, scenery and lighting by Donald Cate, and costumes by Regina Cate. The cast in order of appearance was:

TV ONE	FREDDY MAO
TV TWO	CECILY YAHYA
MERT	MATTHEW LOCRICCHIO
GERT	ROBERTA CALLAHAN
GORF	MARC JACOBS
CHORUS OF STARS	BARBARA ELLIS, JUDY FEIL
SHEPHERD ONE	BRUCE PARRY
SHEPHERD TWO	GARY KRAKOWER
THE BLIND DYKE	PRISCILLA ALDEN
MOTORCYCLE OUTLAW ONE	BRUCE PARRY
MOTORCYCLE OUTLAW TWO	GARY KRAKOWER
THE GIANT PENGUIN	DOUG BROYLES
NAKED GIRL WITH FAIRY WINGS	CAROL ANNE YOUNG
SCRIBE	MATTHEW LOCRICCHIO
WOODCUTTER ONE	BRUCE PARRY
WOODCUTTER TWO	GARY KRAKOWER

Musicians: Daniel Orsborn, Frank Lorca McGee, Donna Howe, Alan Young. Production staff: Michael Wolf, Jim Robinson, Elizabeth Purcell, Terry Peck, Ray Garrett, Kathy Kleinheinz, Carol Anne Young. Administrative staff: Carol Orsborn, Terry Down, Ron Scherl, Al Thacker, Barbara Ellis, Michele Miner, Mary Maywar. Construction and costume crew: Sue Bogosian, Salley Shatford, Michael Derby, Brenda Sparks, Steve Lane, Gladys Svenson. Understudies: John Nesci, Bill Sweatman, David Courier, Saun Ellis. Company manager: Robert Lemon.

GORF

Mert and Gert at home in Thebes. TV One and TV Two watch them.

PROLOGUE

The Ur Gorf Drama

A small part of the stage is used for the prologue. The place is Thebes.

A man and woman, Mert and Gert, sit in overstuffed chairs reading newspapers by the light of two stand-up lamps. Mert and Gert are naked, but there are bands of fur around their bodies in odd places—the arms, the legs, and the waist. The fur is pink and plumey. They wear white gloves.

On the floor are two television sets: TV One and TV Two. The TVs are cabinets with windows in them. Heads, arms, and shoulders can be seen through the screens. They have huge red lips. They rest their arms on the screen ledge and gesticulate and reach out to each other. They shuffle around and dance. TV One has wings on his brow. TV Two has horns on her forehead. They are mindless.

TV ONE: Woweeeee! Try some of this cereal, Honey! It is yummeee yumm! AND IT IS SO CRUNCHY!

[*TV One shuffles a foot or two toward TV Two and holds out a bowl and a spoonful of cereal to her.*]

TV TWO: Woweeeee-wow! [*She hops toward TV One. In reaching with her mouth for a spoon of the cereal held by*

1

TV One, she jiggles the spoon and bowl. Some of the cereal falls out of the bowl onto the floor and rattles and rolls around and makes grating sounds. The cereal is many-colored and the milk with it is purple.]

TV ONE AND TV TWO: My goodness!

MERT [*lowers his paper, looks at the TVs in disgust*]: Jesus! [*He looks back at his paper.*]

GERT [*to Mert without lowering paper*]: What dear?

MERT [*muttering*]: Baseball . . . Baseball . . . I'm reading about baseball . . .

GERT: Oh.

TV ONE [*holding out another spoonful*]: Here, Poopsie, have some more. [*He grins a big, loving grin.*]

[*TV Two hops to TV One, sips a large spoonful of cereal.*]

TV TWO: Yummeee yumm! [*Big, sweet loving grin*]

[*TV One and TV Two kiss each other—a huge, sweet, long lip-kiss.*]

MERT [*quoting the paper*]: Hmmmmmm. . . Says here: "Time and Space got sqwunched together when the scientificos messed around with the snooty-rootian movements." Everything is gonna be different.

GERT: The *what*, dear?

MERT: The snooty-rootian movements—that is the way that little things jiggle around in eternity.

GERT [*turns page*]: Oh.

MERT: Yes, when we feel the big bump then we'll know everything is sqwunched together.

GERT: What will happen then?

MERT: I don't know.

TV ONE [*hugging TV Two*]: YUMMEEEE, YUMMM-EEEE, YUMMEEEE YUMM. . . [*He gives her a big, smooching kiss.*]

TV TWO [*hugging TV One*]: YUMMEEEE, YUMMM-EEEE, YUMMEEEE, YUMM. . . [*He returns the kiss.*]

TV ONE [*winking at TV Two, reaches and takes her hand*]: OH, YOU POOOOOPSIE-DOOOOOPSIE!

TV TWO [*winks at TV One and reaches and takes his other hand*]: YOU POOOOOPSIE-DOOOOOPSIE!

[*Spotlight on TV One and TV Two. Music begins. A rhumba. They dance Very romantic.*]

TV ONE AND TV TWO [*singing*]:
WHEN TIME AND SPACE GET SQUISHED TOGETHER
then it won't matter whether
there's weather
or not!
If hot,
then night is a feather
that strokes on the leather
WHEN TIME AND SPACE GET SQUISHED TOGETHER
whether there's weather or not!
Yummmeeee!

3

Yummeeee!
Yummee!
Yummee!
[*Pause*]
YUM!
[*They kiss.*]

GERT: Mert, did you feel a bump?

MERT: Of course not, Gert. [*He doesn't look up from the paper.*]

TV ONE AND TV TWO:
Whether there's weather or not!
Yummmeeee!
Yummeeee!
Yummee!
Yummee!
[*Pause*]
YUM!
[*They kiss.*]
Whether there's weather or not!

[*The music ends.*]

GERT: I thought I felt a bump!

MERT: Shut the fuck up! [*He rattles the paper—turns the page.*]

[*TVs feed each other cereal and make cooing noises.*]

TV ONE AND TV TWO: Cooo-cooo-cooo-cooo-cooo. . . Cooo. . . [*Etc.*]

MERT: Goddam birds in the eaves again!

4

GERT: We been so lonely since the little Shitfer died.

MERT: Goddamit, pretend there never was the Shitfer! Leave me the fuck alone! I'm reading!

GERT: The poor little Shitfer, he'd be twelve years old today if we hadn'ta got that phone call!

MERT [*paraphrasing*]: Says here there's been mysterious comets and cracks in the earth and big goopy things fell out of the air on top of an orphanage.

GERT [*sentimentally and desperately*]: MERT. . . MERT. . .

MERT: Shuttup! I'LL BREAK YER DAMN FINGERS!

TV ONE AND TV TWO [*continuing*]: Coooo-coooo. . . Coooooo. . . Coooo. . .

[*Enter Gorf. Gorf is purple. He is a flying cock and balls with a face and wings. His pubic hair is a yellow fright wig.*]

GORF [*flies in all adazzle*]: ZOWEEEEEE! WOW, MAN! Hey. . . HEY!?

[*Gorf stops mid-air to listen. He expects answer from the air or off stage.*]

TV ONE [*happily stops cooing*]: Hi, Gorf!

TV TWO: Hi, Gorf!

GORF [*diving down to TVs*]: Hi, TVs. Wha's happening?

[*Mert rattles the paper.*]

5

TV ONE AND TV TWO: We're trying this new cereal and it is really really good and Mert and Gert are reading the paper and Mert was reading about baseball and it was really really good and then Gert asked him what he was doing and he read another part to her about how there's gonna be a big squish when the bump happens and Time and Space get sqwunched together and Mert and Gert wouldn't look at us at all—sometimes I think they don't even like to know we exist—and then they started talkin about the Shitfer again and it made us feel bad so we just pretended that it wasn't happening and everything—and before that we practiced our new rhumba dance with the spotlight and it was really really neat. Hey, would you like to try some cereal? [*Offering a spoonful*]

GORF: No.

[*He flies to the edge of the stage—turns—pauses.*]

Hey, I'm checking on the bump.
There are all kindsa strange rumors about it.
I'm off to find out! [*He blows his horn as he darts off stage.*]
"TARAH! RARAAAH!"

MERT [*reading*]: Says here the Penguins got wiped by the Elks.

GERT: Isn't that hurtful, dear?
Oh my goodness, I'm so concerned about the bump. I hope wherever the Shitfer is that the bump makes him better and happier.
You know that the net of his being was hurled through Time and Space—unfurled so to speak. . . Why he coulda been trapped in the tooth of a mastodon a million years ago. Or he might be out there in the future with his fingertips on the edge of a hundred different stars. My goodness just think about it.

6

Gorf enters to warn Mert and Gert of The Bump.

TV ONE AND TV TWO [*song and dance with spotlight*]:
WHETHER IT'S WASTEFUL OR TASTEFUL
there's always something zestful
about snappy kwappy
KWUNCHEROOS! You'll never have the blues
with snickery
quickery
KWUNCHEROOS!
[*Kiss. Kiss. Kiss.*]
with snickery
quickery
KWUNCHEROOS!
[*Kiss. Kiss. Kiss.*]

MERT [*meditatively, not looking up from the paper*]: Gert, remember that time I went to DEEtroit? [*Pause*] I didn't really get robbed. No, sir. You know the hotel I stayed in? Well it smelled good in there . . . like pretty plastic and rug shampoo, and there was color TVs before we even had one, and there was music on all the different floors of the building. You know what all that done? [*Pause*] I mean it was really exciting. That and just being in the city where so much was happening. I mean it kinda turned me on—sexually—if you know what I mean. Anyway I didn't get hit on the head by robbers on a dark street like I told you. I got to talkin to the elevator operator and he told me dirty stories and I just got overwhelmed with the possibilities of what I could do with that money I was carrying to pay off the mortgage on the tractor.

GERT: My, my that was some time back, wasn't it Mert. What did happen, Mert?

MERT: Well, that elevator operator he was a smart young feller—kinda sneaky-looking but he could hold a drink and he could sure talk good too. He ups and went out and he

8

got me eight girls. Boy, they was really somethin! There was one of every kind. There was two fat ones, there was one skinny as a toothpick, and then there was a blonde and a redhead and one with wiry hair—and there was one that was awful pretty but she didn't have no hands. . . I'll tell you, I get a real picture in the mind when I think about it.

They all took off their clothes. Gert, there was enough clothes there so that I coulda started a used clothing business—and that slick elevator operator he went away with my money. I guess we didn't need that tractor anyway. . .

[*TV One and TV Two shuffle over and stand gaping up at Mert. They hold hands as they gape. Gorf peeps in from mid-air.*]

I had the whole thing figured out. It wasn't easy but I did it. I put my dick in one girl—the one with the real big pretty ears—and I put my mouth right into the pussy of a real hairy girl, then I couldn't see too good but I got a hand in one girl, and a hand in another girl, then the two blonde ones laid the opposite direction on the bed and I put a foot into each of them. They did wiggle and yell because we had been drinkin a lot of wine and beer and whisky. The place smelled good with the smell of the rug shampoo and the turkey carcasses, 'cause we'd been eating a lot of turkeys. And the caviar that was left over smelled good too—and the whipped cream and strawberry shortcake. . .

The last two girls, the one with tattoos on her titties and the one that giggled and talked funny 'cause she'd smoked little cigarettes, climbed right on too and I put a knee into each one of them. Well, we all wiggled and yelled. While I was doing it I thought about the story I was gonna tell you Gert. . . I had some money left afterward. I didn't want to come home with any so I gave it to one of the girls who wanted to buy a little fox with glass eyes to put around her neck to keep her warm in the cold DEEtroit weather.

9

TV ONE AND TV TWO [*admiring the story*]: Wow! WOW! Hey that's neat!

[*Gorf darts across the stage blowing his bugle—* "*TRARAH! TARAAHHH!*"]

[*TV One and TV Two kiss each other—"Smack, smack."*]

GORF [*darting back across stage and off*]: THE BUMP IS COMING—THE BUMP IS COMING!! [*Blowing his horn*]

GERT: Mert, I was lonely while you was on that trip to DEEtroit. There wasn't anybody here with me except the little Shitfer who was only a toddler before he got lost and scattered into all Space and Time. We was here in the snow all by ourselves and the only company we had at first was the troop of cubs the Shitfer belonged to—for which of course I was the den mother. I was so lonely, missing you and thinking about our sorrow after your collect telephone call to tell me you was robbed and beaten up in DEEtroit, that I went to bed. Well, Shitfer and all the cubs was playin and they wanted to be mommy and daddy, so they got into the bed to pretend it was Sunday morning because the big tent in the back, out by the sump, burned down and they wanted to play inside.

I was out of my mind with grief and I couldn't feel anything. I just lay there and all those kids bumped around on top of me. The Shitfer, little rascal, wanted, being a cub, to play mountain and they all climbed around on top of me and then they started playin cave. . . And before you know it they was all goin inside, and in and out, of every part of me. . . The grief had me so bad that I didn't even know it at first. I guess I never had so many kinds of things in and out of me. And it did feel good. The boys went home to tell their daddies—even when I told 'em not to tell anybody. Well, some of the daddies came back and they was

10

pretty excited and said they was gonna tell you, and beat you and me up. . . So I said I'd show the daddies what the cubs had been doin. . . They all liked it when they saw that it was really O.K. and they went and brought back some of their friends too. One of them brought me that bottle of perfume water afterward—and another man gave me two dollars. Most all the men and boys that you know came and it was really interesting and we had quite a time for that few days that you spent hitchhiking back from DEEtroit.

MERT: Well, Gert, that's quite a story.

GERT: Yes, Mert. Your story was interesting too.
Why I wouldn't be any more surprised if a giant hairy elephant sat down right on top of us.

GORF [*blowing his horn fanatically, circling the stage*]: THE BUMP IS COMING! THE BUMP IS COMING! RUN FOR YOUR LIVES THE BUMP IS COMING! [*He circles the stage blowing his horn.*]

[*TV One and TV Two step back and watch Gorf admiringly.*]

TV ONE: My, look at that!

TV TWO: —And listen!

GORF: THE BUMP IS COMING IN THE SHAPE OF A GIANT HAIRY ELEPHANT!

TV ONE AND TV TWO: WOW! WOW! [*Mindlessly pleased*] Listen!

GERT [*reading*]: What do you make of that?

MERT: I don't believe it.

11

[*Huge, hairy bulbous material begins to come down from ceiling slowly and heavily. Off stage horns begin trumpeting in unison with Gorf's horn. The hairy material engulfs Mert and Gert, who ignore it till the very end. They are crushed. The TVs stand watching crying "Wow!" excitedly and hugging each other and giving each other big hugs and kisses. Gorf flies around blowing his horn as Mert and Gert are smothered. A piano duo plays amplified boogie-woogie all over the theater.*]

GIANT AMPLIFIED VOICE: BUMP!!

[*Stars come out and dance. The Stars are nude people in Star costumes with top hats and glitter. They dance in a row with a TV on each end. Gorf flies around playing horn and singing. There are spotlights on Stars, Gorf, and TVs. Spurts of water begin to spray up like fountains at the front of the stage.*]

EVERYBODY [*song and dance*]:
PUT YOUR FINGERS ON A STAR
or you won't get very far
but no matter who you are
YOU
GOTTA
LEARN
to take good care of yourself!

YOU MAY NOT REMEMBER YOU'RE AN ELF
but you gotta keep tellin yourself. . .

[*Everyone in the chorus line kicks legs and throws handfuls of glitter.*]

THAT YOU ARE
more than you think!

12

YOU ARE REAL AND SWEET
and your feet are mighty fleet
and your voice and words are neat
AND
YOU
ARE
more than you think!

BABY, YOU'RE A FAIRY AND AN ELF!
you're an octopus and a star
but no matter who you are
you gotta take good care of yourself!

ALL THE GOLD AND SILVER IN THE WORLD
if you got it all uncurled
and out of the earth
wouldn't be worth
one smile, not one smile, from you. . .
Everybody loves your fingers and toes
—and you got the prettiest nose
SO
you gotta take good care of yourself
CAUSE
you are more than you think. . .

ALL THE GOLD AND SILVER IN THE WORLD. . . [*Etc.*]

[*Trumpets. Ballroom lights flash all through audience.
There are smoke effects, dry-ice vapor, projections on
walls, etc.*

[*Darkness. During the darkness the chairs and props are
suddenly removed. The Abyssinian desert is discovered on
stage.*]

Mert and Gert in the Afterworld.

ACT ONE

Full stage. Night on the Abyssinian desert. There are huge desert plants and snakes. There is a boulder with a door in the front of it. Little curtains are hung in the windows on the door.

The time is the Mythic Era—which begins at the death of Mert and Gert.

Gorf is as he appears in The Ur Gorf Drama. *He is a flying cock and balls.*

TV One and TV Two stand in the shadow of a huge desert plant.

Gorf is in a spotlight. He stands dejected and noble—his wings droop. He is lamenting.

The opening music is for drums, ocarina, and muted bagpipes—mournful in mode with occasional chimes of brass.

GORF: WOE! [*He shakes his wings.*] WOE! [*Shaking wings*] Oh woe! Woe! Woe! Triple woe!

[*Chimes*]

TV ONE [*shuffles to Gorf*]: Gorf! Hey Gorf! Don't be sad.

GORF [*pushes TV One back into the shadow with his wings*]: Shut the fuck up! [*In a grand manner*] WOE! Oh sorrow, that I—I of all creatures should be so. . .

15

TV TWO [*shuffling forward with TV One*]: Yeah, Gorf. Hey Gorf. Come on, don't be sad, Gorf.

GORF [*pushing the TVs aside*]: OH TRAGEDY-Y-Y-Y! OH WOUNDED SORROW THAT I AM BRUISED BY THE DEATH OF FRIENDS. AND THAT THEIR DEATHS ARE ADDED TO MY PRIOR PAINS! OH WOE! Oh Mert! Oh Gert!

TV TWO: Hey, Gorf we can dance for you! Hey Gorf, watch this.

[*TV One and TV Two take out canes and straw hats. The music comes up for a soft-shoe number.*]

TV ONE [*dancing and bowing*]: I am TV One. . .

TV TWO [*dancing and bowing*]: I am TV Two. . .

TV ONE AND TV TWO [*together*]: We'll chase away your cares. . . [*Pause*] We can chase away your. . . [*pause*] blues.

GORF: SHUT UP! SHUT UP! GET THE FUCK AWAY!

[*GORF pushes them back into the shadows of desert plants.*]

TV ONE AND TV TWO: Hey Gorf! We only wanted to cheer you up. You're really neat, Gorf.

GORF [*with an arm over his brow*]: OH LONELINESS OF DESERT CASTAWAY! That I should be blamed for the demise of friends.—That I who tried to warn them with my mystic horn am condemned as their murderer! The city throng does howl for me, to take me to the gallows straight-away! Oh Mert, Oh Gert, that I should be blamed for your

deaths! Gods! GODS! STRIKE THE PARANOIDS WHO
BLAME ME FOR THE DEATHS OF MERT AND GERT
WITH AN ANGRY CRASHRATTLE! [*Thunder and light-
ning*] Tear the skin off them and roll them in the gravel!

Let my horn again sound in the streets of Thebes! [*Gorf
blows his horn: "TRAAAAH-TaraHHHHH."*]

Yeah, let me again soar through the urban air and
brighten city morning with my purple flash. The desert is
too cruel for me! [*He blows his horn.*]

TV ONE AND TV TWO [*shuffling to Gorf*]: Wow! Oh Gorf,
you are really so neat. If you'll play the horn we'll dance,
Gorf.

GORF [*looks around fearfully*]: I hope the townspeople
looking for me didn't hear the horn! I forgot!

[*There are sounds of dogs baying, sirens, shouts. Voices
off stage: "Where is he?" "Where is that prick?"*]

Here they come! Wow! There's no escape unless I disguise
myself!

[*Gorf darts behind the boulder. The TVs give each other
a huge smacking kiss.*]

TV TWO: Hey where did he go? [*Pause*] Oh well.

[*TVs embrace each other.*]

TV ONE: Yummeeee, yummmeeee, yummeeee, numm. . .

TV TWO: Yummeeee, yummmeeee, yummeeee, numm. . .

TV ONE AND TV TWO: Whether there's weather or not!
[*They kiss again.*] Smack! Smack!

17

[TV One and TV Two stand looking into each other's eyes. There is a long silence broken only by a flute tendril of night music. Then everything is still. The moon crosses the sky. Two Shepherds enter. The Shepherds are dressed in burnooses. They are huge and fat and they have long, bloody fangs. They carry crooks.]

SHEPHERD ONE: Hey, Shepherd, look dere is da moon crackin open da darkness of Lady Night.

SHEPHERD TWO: Yeah!

SHEPHERD ONE: We the common people, the workin class, often thinks about poor Gorf.

SHEPHERD TWO: He who is so wrongfullishly accused of duh merder of Mert and Gert. *[He uncorks a bottle, takes a nip—passes it to Shepherd One.]*

SHEPHERD ONE: Yeh. *[Pause]* We know dat Gorf could never commit so bastardly a crime upon his longtime pals.

SHEPHERD TWO: Yeh. Dey was sure crushed flat—Mert and Gert was.

[Shepherd Two takes out a hypodermic needle and shoots up.]

[TV One and TV Two move forward fascinated, watching Shepherd One and Shepherd Two.]

SHEPHERD ONE: But it is the upper class, and the middle class, and the bureau-ocracy, and the scientificos that seek to blame Gorf and thereby off him from da scene.

SHEPHERD TWO: Yeh, and da paranoids!

SHEPHERD ONE: And da paranoids is after him too.

SHEPHERD TWO: Yeh.

SHEPHERD ONE: Jeez, I hope we gets a chance to help him.

SHEPHERD TWO: Yeah, me too.

[*A dead lamb drops out of Shepherd One's burnoose.*]

SHEPHERD ONE: Jeez, lookadat.

SHEPHERD TWO: Yeh, bed and breakfast. [*He picks up the lamb.*]

[*The Shepherds pass off stage. TV One and TV Two follow from a distance—fascinated.*]

TV ONE [*to TV Two*]: Boy, are they neat!

TV TWO: Yeah.

TV ONE AND TV TWO [*following after the Shepherds*]: Hey wait! Wait! Baaaaaaa ba-a-a-a-a. . . [*As they exit they imitate sheep.*]

[*Empty stage. Flute music. Silence. Pause.*]

[*Mert and Gert step out of air onto the top of the boulder. They are as they are in* The Ur Gorf Drama. *They are naked with bands of pink fur in odd places and they wear white gloves. Both of them carry a newspaper. In addition, their hair has become Medusa hair and is filled with writhing snakes. They also have a few streamers of black ribbons tied to them in various places, and there are red gobbets of gore here and there on their bodies.*]

MERT: Gert, this is like the elevator was in the hotel in DEEtroit—you can just step out of the air and be any place you want to be.

GERT: But wouldn't it be nice, Mert, if we could just step out somewhere and find little Shitfer standing there and staring up at us with his big eye. Land sakes, Mert, I even miss Shitfer when I'm dead.

MERT: Listen, Gert, we ARE going to find Shitfer. I've got the feeling. When I get the feeling—we get action.

GERT: Yes, that's right, Mert. What you say is always right, Mert.

MERT: That's right, Gert. But first things have got to come first—even when we are dead, Gert.

GERT: That's right, Mert.

MERT: So, the first thing we've got to do since we've become Assistant Furies is to avenge ourselves against the ruthless murderer that slonked us into the afterworld.

GERT: When I get that giant hairy elephant I am going to twist his tail till he squeals.

MERT: Listen, Gert, it wasn't the giant hairy elephant that killed us. . .

GERT [*pointing to gobbets of blood*]: I hope you don't think this is acne, Mert. Dear, we were sit upon by a giant hairy elephant. So therefore it was a giant hairy elephant that killt us.

MERT: A giant hairy elephant did not think up the idea of coming and sitting on us by himself.

GERT: Then I'll bet his wife thought of it!

MERT: Nope.

GERT: Golly, who would want a giant hairy elephant to sit on us?

MERT: Who was there at the scene of the crime watching and gloating?

GERT: The TVs?

MERT: They was there but it was not them!

GERT: Who?

MERT: He was playing a musical instrument.

GERT: The piano?

MERT: Nope, a magical horn. A magical horn with which our murderer might summon a giant hairy elephant out of the abyss and the chasm created by the sqwunch and the snooty-rootian movements when the great Bump happened.

GERT: Gorf?

MERT: YEP!

GERT: Not Gorf!

MERT: Yes!

GERT: Why did he want to do that?

MERT: So we would not find out where Shitfer has gone!

21

GERT: The winged rat!

MERT: And so he could get the TVs.

GERT: Let's get the little fucker—I'm really mad now!

[*Mert and Gert leap into air and disappear.*]

MERT AND GERT [*their voices in darkness*]: AWAY-Y-Y-Y-Y-Y!

[*Sound of dogs baying, sirens moving away into the distance. Searchers' voices: "Find Gorf!" "Find the little purple shit." Etc.*]

[*Silence*]

[*Pause*]

[*Enter Chorus of Naked Stars. The Naked Stars are as they are in* The Ur Gorf Drama. *They are naked with silver top hats and glitter. They enter carrying flashlights and doing a step that is a cross between a march and a dance. The music is amplified dulcimer, ocarina, boogie-woogie piano, and bells.*]

CHORUS OF NAKED STARS:
WHERE, OH WHERE, IS THE HERO GORF?
HE ISN'T AT THE BARNYARD!
He isn't at the wharf!
Where moon peeps
or flashlight leaps
there is no Gorf.
Great Gorf cannot be seen.
I get the creeps
when I think he might be gone.

What if his wings have gone astutter?
Mayhap we shall no more see him flutter
round the belfries of the town?

Sing down-a-down. Sing down-a-down.

Desert of sorrow.
Desert of grief.

CHORUS: Sandy snakey place beyond belief!

[*Sirens. Baying of hounds. Shouts of searchers: "Where the fuck is he?" Etc.*]

CHORUS LEADER: Hark, the deluded ones search for the noble lord.

[*The Chorus listens and peers with hands shading brows. Sirens diminish into the distance. The Chorus begins high-stepping, and doing kicks. They throw glitter. There are fountain effects.*]

CHORUS: One-kick! Two-kick! Three-kick!
Cheer up Gorf, don't be sad!
At rock bottom
everyone knows you can't be bad!
All of the evil and all of the rotten
never should have gotten
on your tail.
Great love will not fail
to win your case.
Gorf,
Gorf,
show your wings and face.
Great love will not fail
to win your case!
One-kick! Two-kick! Three-kick! [*Etc.*]

[*The Chorus does high-kicks off stage in the midst of fountains and flickering lights. They throw glitter. Pause. Silence. Tendril of flute music. Dawn begins to break. Gorf steps from behind the boulder. He is dressed in a huge filmy nightgown and has several wigs on in odd places. His face is made up with rouge.*]

GORF [*with a little leap*]: No one will recognize me in the guise of woman. [*Pause. Pirouette. He brushes at his hair.*] I have determined to re-enter Thebes in the form of girl. There will I find the murderers of Mert and Gert—the monstrous ones who caused the giant hairy elephant to sit upon them when the Bump happened. But soft—dawn breaks! Before the peep of Phoebus as I lay asleep in womanly dress my soul was gentled by a band of wandering sprites, in the shape of Stars, that sang to me. I was dreaming that I had the paranoids and murderers and I choked them one by one watching the veins burst bulbously upon their faces. And aye sweet it was to watch them cry out and writhe!—Sweet the humility with which I strangled them and tortured their children. . . [*Pause*] Methinks a higher thought appeared in shape of those nightly suns that we call Stars and they did remind me of my business in the town. . . And then I awoke all awonder and determined to go to Thebes and bring my dream to action. So with the convenience of this womanly garb I will do so. . .

[*Gorf sees a snake and grabs it.*]

Wow! [*He sees more snakes and grabs them.*] MORE! [*Loud hissings*] MORE! MORE!

I'll just put these snakes in this basket. When I get to Thebes I'll sell them. The populace will think that I am a harmless snake girl peddling my wares.

24

[*The snakes revive with hissings and try to get out of basket.*]

If I fly to Thebes they will recognize me and know I am Gorf. Therefore I will hitchhike. . .

[*He sticks his thumb out.*]

[*He hums in falsetto to the tune of "Cockles and Mussels."*] Singing vipers and rattlers and huge giant boas. . . Singing vipers and pythons . . . alive—alive oh. . .

[*Mert and Gert run across the stage. They do not give Gorf a second look.*]

My disguise works. The avenging Assistant Furies do not know me. Gee, they remind me of Mert and Gert.
[*He hums.*] Singing pythons and boas. . . alive—alive oh. . . [*Etc.*]

[*Sound of a motorcycle approaching. A motorcycle driven by the Blind Dyke roars onto stage. The chopper pulls to a screeching halt in front of Gorf. The Blind Dyke weighs five hundred pounds, wears black glasses and a leather jacket, and has a crewcut. The Blind Dyke leaps off her chopper and gropes with her arms out for Gorf. Her voice is huge and deep.*]

BLIND DYKE: HEY. . . HEY, PRETTY LITTLE MISSY, I HEARD YOU SINGING. IT IS I—THE BLIND DYKE —ON MY WAY TO DELIVER SOME PARTS TO THE AUTO REPAIR SHOPS IN THEBES. I HEARD YA SINGING. [*She grasps Gorf by the negligee.*] CAN I GIVE YA A RIDE? [*Gorf tries to run and fly but the Blind Dyke has a firm grip on the nightgown. She grabs Gorf, stroking his various wigs.*] BY HEAVEN, THAT'S SURE A LOT OF HEADS YOU GOT, MISSY!

The Blind Dyke grasps Gorf—who is disguised as
"Gorfetta."

GORF [*squealing*]: Help! Help!

BLIND DYKE: There, there little thing. [*Salivates*]

[*Gorf struggles.*]

GORF [*in falsetto*]: I'm waiting for my boyfriend. He's coming back from hunting. He wanted me to meet him right here. He has his twelve-gauge shotgun with him.

[*Gorf struggles free and escapes for a moment.*]

BLIND DYKE: OOOOOOOPS! [*Melodiously*] Where are you-ooo?

[*The Blind Dyke listens carefully—she runs at Gorf. Gorf stops. The Blind Dyke listens. Gorf makes a little noise. The Blind Dyke runs at Gorf with arms out. The Blind Dyke misses. She listens. The snakes hiss. The Blind Dyke runs at the snakes' hissing.*]

GORF [*throws his falsetto voice like a ventriloquist*]:—I'm over here. . .

[*The Blind Dyke runs at Gorf—she almost gets him. She listens. He breathes. She grasps him.*]

GORF: Eeeeeeek!

BLIND DYKE: THERE, THERE, LITTLE MISSY! DON'T TREMBLE—WE'LL JUST RIDE INTO THEBES TO-GETHER.

GORF:—But my boyfriend!

27

BLIND DYKE: THAT'S ALL RIGHT! I KNOW WHAT TO DO WITH BOYFRIENDS! [*She devastates an imaginary boyfriend with karate chop.*] HHHHHHHHA! HAYEE! [*Several huge desert plants fall over.*]

[*Two incredible rough Outlaw Motorcyclists run onto the stage. They are in leather and chrome chains.*]

OUTLAW MOTORCYCLIST ONE: HEY, CRUNCH! LOOK, CRUNCH, IT IS THE BLIND DYKE! HEY, MAN, IT IS THE BLIND DYKE WITH SOME WEIRD LOOKIN BROAD IN A NIGHTGOWN. HEY, MAN THIS IS OUR CHANCE TO KILL THE BLIND DYKE, STEAL HER BIKE, AND RAPE THE BROAD! HEY, MAN, OH HAPPY DAY!

OUTLAW MOTORCYCLIST TWO: YEH, SLUG, LET'S GET HER!

OUTLAW MOTORCYCLIST ONE: SURE MAN, YOU GET BEHIND HER!

[*The Blind Dyke drops Gorf, who lies on the desert caught up in his wigs and negligee. The Blind Dyke listens and gropes the air. With bellows and shouts the Outlaw Motorcyclists attack.*]

OUTLAW MOTORCYCLISTS: KILL HER! MURDER HER! OH HAPPY DAY! KILL THE BLIND DYKE!

[*The Blind Dyke attacks—she gouges the eye out of one Outlaw Motorcyclist and swallows it whole. He runs off screaming.*]

BLIND DYKE: DASTARD MALES!

[*She tears the arm off the other Outlaw Motorcyclist and beats him off stage with it amidst splashing blood. The terrified screams of the Outlaw Motorcyclists disappear into distance.*]

BLIND DYKE: THUNDERING SAPPHO, I HATE PECK-ERS AND BALLS!

[*The Blind Dyke feels around desert floor for Gorf, who tries to writhe away. She listens, hears Gorf breathe, and gets closer. Gorf tries desperately to writhe away but is caught in the nightgown. The Blind Dyke grabs Gorf and picks him up. She gives him a huge kiss on the wigs, and fingers his negligee passionately.*]

BLIND DYKE: THERE, THERE, MISSY, EVERYTHING IS GONNA BE ALL RIGHT!

[*In the process of groping Gorf she takes hold of a giant snake.*]

DROOLING PUSSIES, IT'S A PECKER! [*She bites the snake in half.*] GNAWMF! Oh heck it was just a harmless giant python. I THOUGHT IT WAS A PECKER! Well, maybe it was a boy snake and then it don't matter.

GORF [*in higher falsetto*]: Right you are, big Blind Dyke.

[*Blind Dyke cradles Gorf like a baby.*]

BLIND DYKE: What is your name little lady?

GORF: Gorfetta! My name is Gorfetta, kind Blind Dyke. I am fourteen years old and a sweet virgin.

29

The Blind Dyke tears the arm off an Outlaw Motor-cyclist. She beats him with it amidst splashing blood.

BLIND DYKE [SONG]:
GORFETTA, GORFETTA, what a sweet name is Gorfette.
What a pretty little hand you have.
It is made to throw confetti.
What pretty little toes you have
they remind me of spaghetti.
Let me kiss you on the cheek.
I will hug you till you squeak.
Gorfetta,
Gorfetta,
GORFETTE. . .

GORF [*trying to keep his wigs on*]: Ooooh, what an impetuous thing you are, Blind Dyke.

BLIND DYKE: Gorfetta, I am infatuated. You must be mine!

GORF: O-o-o-o-o-oh, but Blind Dyke, you are a woman. How could that be—and how could that happen?

BLIND DYKE: There are mysteries, Gorfette, that will be revealed to you. Never again will you be blue. The tongue of the Blind Dyke promises true.

GORF: Woo-woo!

BLIND DYKE: I will take you to my secret penthouse high above Thebes town—we'll have our marriage feast of divinity and pink caviar. I'll show you my collection of pickled cocks and balls!

GORF: Pickled cocks and balls?

BLIND DYKE: Don't worry my little sweet, they won't hurt you. They are cut off and float in big barrels of vinegar. I've got more cocks and balls than any other dyke in Greece.

31

Hey, little Gorfetta, don't wiggle!

GORF: Oh, I am so anxious. Let's hurry to Thebes.

BLIND DYKE: Can't wait to see my collection?

GORF: Yes, to view it will be a visual confection.

BLIND DYKE: My dear!

GORF: Hurry, hurry, I'm all atremble.

BLIND DYKE: I thought I felt you shakin'.

GORF: Wheeeeeeeeeeee!

BLIND DYKE: DON'T FORGIT YER SNAKES! AWAY
WE GO!

[*Her chopper roars off stage with sparks and smoke, Gorf
in the sidecar.*]

[*Long pause. Tendril of flute music. The door in the
boulder opens. A Giant Penguin slowly walks to front
center stage. Pause.*]

GIANT PENGUIN: Ahem. . . Though I appear to be a giant
penguin, in fact I am a particle of The Shitfer. [*Pause*] In
the Pre-Mythic days before the demise of Mert and Gert,
when every spirit was a real thing, then—I a particle of The
Shitfer—was united with the true and only Shitfer.
Now I must wander in this mythic spirit shape through
the quaverings made by the giant Bump when the chasm
opened and the hairy elephant sat on Mert and Gert.
Ahem. . . Everything tends toward one-ness. [*Pause*] As
I find the other particles of The Shitfer we will join together.

The Blind Dyke prepares to speed away on her chopper with "Gorfetta."

When the True Shifter is reconstituted into one Whole, then the Pre-Mythic days will come into being again. Then all will be real—as it was before. All will be real. Again there will be true problems and true loves. . .

[*The Giant Penguin takes one more step forward. Music begins for the song. The music is made by drums, violins, bells, and muted bagpipes.*]

[*Song*] AGAIN THERE WILL BE TRUE PROBLEMS AND TRUE LOVES. . .

[*Half of the Chorus of Naked Stars dances in from each side of the stage. The Chorus joins the song.*]

CHORUS: AGAIN THERE WILL BE TRUE PROBLEMS AND TRUE LOVES. . .

GIANT PENGUIN [*basso profundo*]: There will be rainbow bears and naked doves. . .

CHORUS [*tenor*]: There will be rainbow bears and naked doves. . .

GIANT PENGUIN: Then I. . .

CHORUS [*with a high-kick*]: Then I. . .

GIANT PENGUIN: Shall dance upon immortal ice. . .

CHORUS: Shall dance upon immortal ice. . .

GIANT PENGUIN:
    Everything and everyone will happen in a trice.
We shall supercede the age of lead with the age that's nice.

There will be true problems and true loves.
There will be rainbow bears and naked doves.
The movements of the dimensions
shall be freed of the condescensions
that matter requires of them.

CHORUS: That matter requires of them.

GIANT PENGUIN AND CHORUS:
There will be true problems and true loves.
There will be rainbow bears and naked doves.
The movements of dimensions
shall be freed of the condescensions
that matter still requires of them. . .
Everything and everyone will happen in a trice. . .
Everything and everyone will happen in a trice. . .

GIANT PENGUIN: We will march on Thebes and find the other particles of The Shitfer. . . ! EVERYTHING WILL BE JOINED TOGETHER!

CHORUS: HURRAH!

[*The TVs run on stage.*]

TV ONE AND TV TWO: Listen!

CHORUS: WE WILL MARCH ON THEBES AND FIND THE OTHER PARTICLES OF THE SHITFER! Everything will be joined together. Everything and everyone will happen in a trice!

[*The Chorus is joined by drums and fifes. The Giant Penguin and Chorus march off stage. TV One and TV Two rush after them as they depart.*]

TV ONE AND TV TWO: Wait for us! Hey, wait for us Chorus of Naked Stars and Giant Penguin. Hey we wanna see The Shitfer too. Hey, wait. Hey, are there really going to be true problems and true loves?

 END OF ACT ONE—CURTAIN

ACT TWO

The Great Alchemical Act

Various localities in the vicinity of Thebes and Abyssinia. The time is the Mythic Era following the deaths of Mert and Gert.

Scene One

[*Gorf is flying through the dark sky. Clouds are passing. Gorf is dressed in negligee and is in dishabille. He carries the basket of writhing snakes. A wig drops from him as he flies.*]

GORF [*blowing horn*]: "TARAHHHHH! TRATAR-AHHHHH! TA-TA-ROOOOOOH! TAHREEEEEEEEEE-EEEEEEEEEH!"

OH JOYOUS FREEDOM! FREEDOM! Liberty! The Blind Dyke is far below and I wing toward Thebes. OH MERT, OH GERT, I'LL FIND THY MURDERERS AND AVENGE THEE! The name of Gorf again shall ring proud and free above the ancient vineyards where the grape and olive swell. The secret tyrant murderers shall feel the slice of my wingtip on their brows.

37

The Naked Girl with Fairy Wings dictates to the Scribe.

When the Blind Dyke groped me—leaning to the sidecar where I was held helpless captive—I bashed her in the snoot with this snakey basket. As she drew back with her blind orbs whirling in her chthonic skull she missed the road. A cave appeared before us and the motorcycle careened within. I leaped into the air upon my pinions as the engined beast struck the Stygian wall. There was silence there as I flew out—and clouds of smokey dust such as those oft seen from Aetna's top on an augured day.

[*Gorf zooms on—clouds pass. Gorf blows his horn: "Trahhhh! Tarahhhh!" Etc.*]

It is me, GORF! ME! AND FREE!

[*He blows his horn.*]

The ancient prophesy that proclaims: "Gorf of all shall bring the godlike to a glowing gleam" shall be proved this day. Stars are my friends and clouds are my citadels.

[*Throwing snakes from basket*] Go, oh limbless brethren, tell the People of the Snake that Gorf, great Gorf, is free and asks their company in the revenge of Mert and Gert. Go! Go!

Scene Two

[*Blackness. Then the Blind Dyke crashes across stage through a thunderstorm. She travels in the same direction as Gorf. Her feet make huge stomping sounds. She cries out in wails of sadness and loss. She moves slowly against the crashing wind. Mert and Gert dash across the stage, passing the Blind Dyke going in the opposite direction.*]

39

MERT AND GERT [*in a ghostly voice*]: WOOOOOOOOOO-OOooooo! [*They continue off.*]

BLIND DYKE: SORROW! SORROW! Oh, Mistress Gorfette —I will find you and you will love me yet. My chopper is smashed against the cavern wall—and your dear little body is gone! I could not find you. Even where the Stygian dark meant not a jot to me—for I dwell in swartness—I could not find you! I could not hear you breathe.

[*Song*]

I COULD NOT FIND YOU!
I COULD NOT HEAR YOU BREATHE!
Even in the darkness I could not hear your bosom heave!
Gorfette, Gorfette I'll hold your dear
little fingers yet.
In the cavern black, with only ears to see the light,
and holding my breath
with all my thoughts contrite
I could not hear
I could not hear
I could not hear . . . Gorfette.
[Crashes of thunder—lightning effects]

[*Pause*] Back to Thebes! With the tribe of tribads I'll come back and find Gorfette. [*Pause*] Strange, in the moment when I lay there stunned—right after the chopper crashed into the stalagmite and before the sidecar tire blew—I heard wings of some cavern creature beating in the air. Oh well, perhaps it was some huge bat or owl. But mayhap I heard a horn blow in the storm outside the cave as I lay there! It must have been hallucination. . . On to Thebes. . . [*Wailing*] Gorrrrrfette. . . GORRRRRRFETTE. . .

[*Mert and Gert rush by going in same direction as the Blind Dyke. They rush past her without stopping.*]

MERT AND GERT:
WOOOOOOOOOOOOOOOOOOOOOOOOOOOOOOOOO!
[*They rush off.*]

GERT: Hey Mert, just a minute. . . Wait up!

MERT [*off stage*]: WOOOOOOOooooooooooo. . .

BLIND DYKE [*exiting*]: GORFETTAAAAAAAAaaaaaa. . .

Scene Three

[*Blackness. Gorf flies through the night sky—clouds pass.
There is wind whistling and music.*]

GORF [*throwing the last of the wigs away*]: Away, oh
signs of woman's nature. No longer do I need disguise! I
GORF! I AM! I BREATHE! I'M FREE! OH MERT, OH
GERT, I WILL FIND YOUR MURDERERS! I'll split the
Bump and clamber down the path to Erebus to find the
villains! [*He blows his horn: TARAHHHHH! Etc.*]

Scene Four

[*The Blind Dyke crashes across stage going in the direction of Thebes. She wails: "Gorfette. . . Gorfette. . ." The
Blind Dyke exits.*

[*TV One and TV Two enter.*]

TV ONE: Look, look, TV Two, there is the Blind Dyke.
Hey look at her run—right through the storm scene and
everything.

TV TWO: Yes, wow, the Blind Dyke is really neat.

[*The TVs stop at center stage and stare into each other's eyes. They give each other a big kiss*.]

TV ONE: Yummeeee, yummmeeee, yummeeee, numm. . .

TV TWO: Nummeeee, nummmeeee, nummeeee, numm. . .

TV ONE AND TV TWO [*kissing*]: SMACK! SMACK! Whether there's weather or not!

TV TWO: Oh, wow, that was really neat!

TV ONE: Really, really, really neat?

TV ONE AND TV TWO [*kissing*]: SMACK! SMACK! Whether there's weather or not!

[*Pause. The storm goes away. Rainbows*]

TV TWO: The Blind Dyke is really neat.

TV ONE: Yes, she really is neat. I like Gorf too. Do you like Gorf as much as I do?

TV TWO: Gorf and the Blind Dyke are both really super neat.

TV ONE: Do you remember when we were eating the many-colored cereal in *The Ur Gorf Drama* and Mert and Gert were reading the newspapers and Mert and Gert weren't saying anything to us and were trying to pretend that we weren't there because we remind them of Shitfer and they feel bad about Shitfer being all tossed around everywhere in Time and Space so that he is everywhere at once and that

42

was right before Mert told Gert the story about how he went to DEEtroit with the money for the mortgage on the tractor?

TV TWO: Yes, and that was right before Gert told Mert all about how Shitfer had the cub troop over and they played hide-everything-and-find-it-again under the bedcovers with her and then they went home and told their daddies and their daddies came and saw Gert and one of them gave her a bottle of rose water (the one that is still there on the lampstand by the chair where she sits) and another daddy gave her two dollars and then Gorf came in blowing his horn and yelling about the Bump and the big hairy elephant came and sat down on top of Mert and Gert.

TV ONE: Yes, that's right.

TV ONE AND TV TWO: Whether there's weather or not! [*They kiss.*] SMACK! SMACK!

TV ONE: Well, I wasn't really reading the back page of Gert's newspaper because we were eating the cereal and singing but I couldn't help noticing an article on the back about a prophesy regarding Gorf.

TV TWO: Oh, wow, that's neat. A prophesy regarding Gorf.

TV ONE: Yes.

[*The TVs embrace and kiss with smacks.*]

TV ONE AND TV TWO: Yummeeee, yummmeeee, yummeeee, yumm. . . Nummeeee, nummmeeee, nummeeee, numm. . . Whether there's weather or not! SMACK! SMACK! [*They look into each other's eyes.*]

TV TWO: What did it say?

43

TV ONE: The article about the prophesy regarding Gorf said that the prophesy said: "Gorf of all shall bring the god-like to a glowing gleam." [*A small pink smoke effect goes off.*] That's what the article said.

TV TWO [*clapping hands*]: Oh wow! [*Repeating*] "GORF OF ALL SHALL BRING THE GODLIKE TO A GLOW-ING GLEAM." [*Small pink smoke effect*] Oh, wow, that's really neat. That's really, really neat.

TV ONE [*proudly*]: "GORF OF ALL SHALL BRING THE GODLIKE TO A GLOWING GLEAM." [*Small pink smoke effect*]

TV TWO: Neat!

TV ONE AND TV TWO [*together*]: "GORF OF ALL SHALL BRING THE GODLIKE TO A GLOWING GLEAM." [*Larger pink smoke effect*]

TV TWO: Shall we dance now?

TV ONE: The newspaper article on the back page said some other things too.

TV TWO: Neat! [*Clapping hands*] What?

TV ONE: It said that Gorf is going to bring all of the particles of the Shitfer back together and make one whole Great Shitfer again. I wanted to tell Mert and Gert about the article. I thought they might be interested. Then you and I got busy doing some other things and Gorf came in and Mert and Gert told their stories and the giant hairy elephant sat on them.

TV TWO: Oh, that's neat. Wow!

[*Music strikes up. TV One and TV Two whip out straw hats and canes. They begin a soft-shoe song and dance.*]

TV ONE [*dancing and bowing*]: I am TV One. . .

TV TWO [*dancing and bowing*]: I am TV Two. . .

TV ONE AND TV TWO:
>We'll chase away your cares. . .
>We can chase away your blues.
>Life's a golden feather
>blowing on the heather. . .
>
>Your troubles are a fountain
>bubbling from a mountain.
>Little tiny flowers
>growing through the hours
>are higher than the towers
>reflected in your eyes. . .
>[*Pause, bow, etc.*]
>. . .Are higher than the towers
>reflected in your eyes. . .

[*Shepherd One and Shepherd Two crash on stage. They are running in great fear, stamping on heavy feet, and looking behind them. They careen into TV One and TV Two and bowl them over. The dead sheep goes flying.*]

SHEPHERD ONE [*rubbing his head*]: Hey! WHAT DUH FUCK!

SHEPHERD TWO: YEH, WHAT DUH FUCK?

TV ONE [*happily*]: Oh wow! Look at them!

TV TWO: Wow!

TV ONE AND TV TWO [*embracing and kissing*]: SMACK! SMACK!

SHEPHERD TWO [*to Shepherd One*]: HEY MAN, LET'S HURRY AND GET OUTTA HERE. MAN, DAT WAS REALLY TERRIFYING!

TV ONE: Dear sir, what terrifies you?

SHEPHERD ONE [*to Shepherd Two*]: HEY, MAN, LET'S GRAB DA SHEEP AND BEAT OUR FEET RIGHT ON OUT!

TV TWO: Shepherd, whither goest thou?

[*The Shepherds do not notice or speak to the TVs.*]

SHEPHERD TWO: I'M OUTTA BREATH, MAN.

SHEPHERD ONE: IT IS A DAY OF BAD OMENS. FOIST WE SEES A ONE-ARMED MOTORCYCLIST RUNNING DOWN THE ROAD SPOUTIN BLOOD OUTTA HIS STUMP—AND HE'S BEING FOLLOWED BY A ONE-EYED MOTORCYCLIST ALSO RUNNING. . .

SHEPHERD TWO [*catching his breath*]: Puff. Puff. YEAH. MAN, DAT IS NOT EXACTLY A GOOD OMEN BUT DE NEXT TING REALLY PUT ME IN A FRAME OF MIND FOR RUNNING.

SHEPHERD ONE: YEAH, SCARCELY DID WE SEE THAT WHEN WE BEHELD A GIANT GOD—DE VULTURE GOD ALL BLACK AND SCAREY WIT WEBBY FEET—AND AROUND HIM WAS DANCING GIANT GLOWWORMS AND THEY WAS SINGING AND JIVING AND COMING DOWN THE ROAD RIGHT TO-

WARD US—AND DOING TINGS DAT LOOKED LIKE HIGH-KICKS!

SHEPHERD TWO: I TINK DEY IS AFTER US FOR RIPPING OFF DIS HERE SHEEP . . .

SHEPHERD ONE: DROP IT DERE, MAN. LET'S SPLIT. [*He drops the sheep on the stage.*]

[*The Shepherds run off stage puffing.*]

TV ONE AND TV TWO [*kissing, embracing*]: SMACK! SMACK!

TV ONE [*noticing the sheep*]: Look at that.

TV TWO: Hey, that is neat! Wow!

TV ONE [*shouting off stage*]: Oh, Shepherds, you forgot your sheep.

TV TWO: Shepherds, here is your sheep. . .

TV ONE AND TV TWO [*running after the Shepherds and carrying the sheep*]: Oh, SHEPHERDS, YOU FORGOT SOMETHING. . . Oh, wait for us. . . Hey, Shepherds. . .

[*Blackness*]

Scene Five

[*Gorf is standing on a pinnacle overlooking a mountain range with Thebes visible in the distance.*]

GORF: Strange that I should have this feeling. Odd that this thrill should send its tendrils through the woe that soaks

47

my body. I cannot think except that the prophesy does enter into my mind. Can it be—is it possible—that this is the day the prophesy is to be fulfilled?

"GORF OF ALL SHALL BRING THE GODLIKE TO A GLOWING GLEAM." [*Small pink smoke effect*] And there were other strange words spoken. There were some intimations about a giant bird. . . There were whisperings about a woman who was not a woman. . . [*Pause*] Something in my thoughts tries to speak to me. . . [*Pause*] And yet I cannot grasp it! [*Pause*] Oh well, this noble view thrills my soul with highest thoughts of pure revenge. —Oh Mert, oh Gert! Would that you were here with me!

[*Gorf takes out his mystic horn and blows it. The mountains and vales re-echo.*]

"TAH-RAHHHHHHHH!"
"TAH-ROOOOOOOOOO!"
"Tah-reeeeeeeee-tah-rahhhhhhh!"

[*Voices of Mert and Gert are tangled with the wind.*]

MERT AND GERT VOICES: WE SHALL GET THEE GORF! FOUL MURDERER!

GORF: Hark, do I hear voices on the wind? Oh no, it cannot be for I am here upon these solitary crags where there is no company. Here and only here can my spirit run free. I'll rest a while and then be on to Thebes.

[*Meditative pause*]

Before I go I must sort the voices speaking in my soul. [*Long pause*] There were strange auguries and proclamations connected with the prophesy. Around my cradle it was spoken that it would be I who saw the changing of the worlds—and then see them change back again. It was said that I would see the change from real to mythical. [*Pause*] And that the death of friends would emblemize the change of reality to dream. An old crone suspected by many to be a goddess looked into my cradle and said that it would be I who would bring back the real in time of mythos. . .

BUT OH HOW STRANGE—EVERYTHING SWIRLS!

Ah, there it grows calm again. . . [*Pause*]

Others said that I would be responsible for drawing strange creatures together to make a greater whole than existed before. But there are great wholes and there are large holes. To fill the whole with holes or the hole with big wholes might be a noble task—and surely it is made for one who is more than man. . . [*Pause*] But could it be so for one who is more than woman? My senses twirl! My horn! My horn!

"TAH-RAHHHH!"

"TAH-ROOOOOOOOOOH!"

"TAH-REEEEEEEEEEEEEH!"

[*He peers down.*] But hark! Strange things happen there below on the many roads to Thebes. Figures run one way and another! There is great movement. I must study what is happening.

[*Huge red tentacles appear over the edge of the pinnacle behind Gorf and they reach, menacing him. Gorf turns.*]

What?! GADZOOKS!

Scene Six

[*A Naked Girl with Fairy Wings sits on a rock looking down into a stream. A bearded Scribe in a robe sits with his back against a rock—he writes with a feather pen.*]

49

NAKED GIRL: And so . . . since I sit here almost every day on this rock halfway between Abyssinia and Thebes. . . [*Pause*]

SCRIBE [*writing*]: ". . .halfway between Abyssinia and Thebes. . ."

NAKED GIRL: I cannot help noticing that the vibrations in the rock. . . No wait, say *stone* and not rock . . . in the *stone* are every day becoming more and more. . .

SCRIBE: ". . .every day becoming more and more. . ."

NAKED GIRL: Well, what I mean to say. . .

SCRIBE: "Well, what I mean to say. . ."

NAKED GIRL: No! No!

SCRIBE: No?

NAKED GIRL: Stop! Go back!

SCRIBE: O.K. ". . .in the rock, er, *stone* are every day becoming more and more. . ."

NAKED GIRL: More and more like the jiggle-vibrations caused by the snooty-rootian. . .

SCRIBE [*carefully and slowly*]: ". . .snooty-rootian. . ."

NAKED GIRL: Snooty-rootian movements—they are more and more like the jiggle-vibrations caused by the snooty-rootian movements that happened right before. . .

SCRIBE: ". . .that happened right before. . ."

NAKED GIRL: . . .that happened right before the huge Bump when Time and Space were sqwunched together and the giant hairy elephant sat on Mert and Gert. . .

[*The Scribe jumps up and grabs his hat.*]

SCRIBE: I'm getting out of here!

[*The Scribe runs off stage. Two Woodcutters walk across the stage conversing. The Naked Girl with Fairy Wings watches from her rock as they pass.*]

WOODCUTTER ONE: I tell you things is really different.

WOODCUTTER TWO: Yeah, it is all these intense vibrations and such.

WOODCUTTER ONE: Something is gonna happen.

WOODCUTTER TWO: Yeah boy!

WOODCUTTER ONE: It feels just like it did before the big Bump when Mert and Gert were sit upon by the giant hairy elephant.

WOODCUTTER TWO: Yeah.

WOODCUTTER ONE: Yeah.

WOODCUTTER TWO: You can even feel it right out here in the middle of nowhere.

WOODCUTTER ONE: Yeah.

WOODCUTTER TWO: Yeah.

WOODCUTTER ONE: Makes me nervous.

WOODCUTTER TWO: Yeah boy!

WOODCUTTER ONE: I'm scared.

[*The Naked Girl watches them exit as her fairy wings flutter. Blackness.*]

Scene Seven

[*Gorf on the pinnacle fighting the Mountain Octopus whose great red tentacles reach gropingly for him. Gorf beats off the Mountain Octopus with beautiful swordsmanship—using his mystic horn as a weapon.*]

GORF: TAKE THAT, FOUL MOUNTAIN OCTOPUS!

[*He swordfights with the monster. The beast forces Gorf to the precipice. With a deft stroke Gorf drives the Mountain Octopus back again. The fight continues. Through his superior gifts Gorf—at last—wins.*]

GORF: WRETCHED BEAST!

[*The creature is forced over the edge and plummets to the valley below. Falling it gives the death cry of the Mountain Octopus.*]

MOUNTAIN OCTOPUS: HAYEEEEEEEEEEEEEEEEE-e-e-e-e-e-e-eeeeeeeeee!

GORF [*meditatively*]: Strange things are happening. This is like the time right before the Bump—a time when the nocturnal mountain octopi came out by daylight. [*Pause*] New philosophies are born on days like these. [*He falls into a dark study.*]

Scene Eight

[*The Blind Dyke stumbles across a landscape of bones in semidarkness.*]

BLIND DYKE [*crying out against the wind*]: GORFETTA-A-A-A-A-A-A. . . Hah, I must rest here in this charnel house of bones. Here where the vulture dwells. [*She seats herself on a huge bone.*] Always, always will I seek my dear Gorfette until I find her. [*She cries out.*] GORFETTE. . . ! GORFETTA! When I return with the tribe of tribads we will find Gorfette and then we will dance and sing the Sapphic song and lisp our Lesbic liturgies together. Ah, sweet and happy future. Ahh, Gorfette. . .
[*Song*]
       OH SWEET AND HAPPY FUTURE
WHEN OUR LOVE COMES OUT OF CLOTURE. . .

[*As the Blind Dyke begins the dance that accompanies the song she steps upon one of the wigs that Gorf had been wearing.*]

Hark, what is this strange, soft thing beneath my foot in this osseous landscape—in this foul spot that is the empery of vultures. A frightened thrill of apprehension jiggles through my body. I will not feel it! I will continue with my song. My senses do not recognize it! I am glad that my eyes cannot tell me. Just this once do I rejoice in blindness!

[*The Blind Dyke weeps and clutches the wig to her chest. She tries to sing but breaks down.*]

The Blind Dyke stumbling across the landscape of bones.

[*Song*]
WHEN OUR LOVE COMES OUT OF CLOTURE. . .
OH, OUR SWEET AND HAPPY FUTURE. . .

OH EARTH BREAK OPEN AND WEEP! [*She sniffs the wig*.] I know this sweet beloved scent. I know this virgin musk. I recognize the odor of my dearest, dear Gorfette. [*She bellows with sorrow*.] EVEN WITH THE BLACKNESS IN MY EYES I GET A PICTURE IN MY MIND OF WHAT DID TRULY HAPPEN TO MY DEAR GORFETTE. OH, GODDESSES AVENGE ME! I'M REALLY MAD!

[*Acting in pantomine*] My loveliest, dearest, dear Gorfette was flung clean from my sidecar. . . She lay dazed upon a ledge in the cavern like a nurseling bat as I searched for her. The sound I heard of wings was that of a giant vulture searching for its foul dinner. . . Oh horror—it watched my dazed Gorfette! In my searching I walked out into the storm. The wretched vulture waited in the cave. Gorfette felt the lovely gleam of gentle consciousness return to her. As I wandered one way she wandered another into these hills. When she came upon this aerie of the villain Vulture King she fell with exhaustion. "Blind Dyke. . ." she cried, "Blind Dyke, I cry to you, take me to your place in Thebes. . ." And then the vulgar Vulture King and all his kindred fell upon her and left naught upon this hill except her precious hair. . .

[*Song*]
  THERE'S NAUGHT UPON THIS HILL
    EXCEPT HER PRECIOUS HAIR.
      Gone, gone is Gorfette!
    The pretty little hand she had
     that was made to throw confetti. . .
  Gone, gone are the pretty little toes she had
      that reminded me of spaghetti. . .
        I kiss,
        I KISS. . .
        I KISS. . .

55

I KISS THIS PRECIOUS HAIR
AND BID GOODBYE TO ALL THAT'S FAIR!

[*Mert and Gert cross the stage—one from each side. They cry, "WOOOOOOOOOOOOOOOOOOOOOoooooooo-oooo. . ."*]

[*Shepherd One rushes on stage.*]

SHEPHERD ONE [*puff, puff*]: HOLY GEE, ONE TING I WANTA DO IS GET OUTTA DIS PLACE AND AS FAR AWAY FROM THE GIANT VULTURE GOD AS I CAN GET! Woo-wee, DIS IS SCAREY!

[*The Blind Dyke listens carefully, locates him, and leaps on Shepherd One. She crushes him under her. She grasps him by the throat and crotch.*]

BLIND DYKE: GOTCHA!

SHEPHERD ONE: HEY, LEMME OUTTA HERE! HELP! HELP!

BLIND DYKE: ONE WIGGLE OUT OF YOU, AND I, THE BLIND DYKE, WILL TEAR YOUR CROTCH OUT AND ADD IT TO MY COLLECTION OF PICKLED WHANGS!

SHEPHERD ONE: HELP, LEMME GO! LEMME GO! ALL I WANT TO DO IS GET OUTTA HERE, MISS BLIND DYKE!

BLIND DYKE: LEAD ME TO THE VULTURE KING!

SHEPHERD ONE: ANYTHING BUT DAT! I IS RUNNING AWAY FROM HIM!

[*The Blind Dyke gives Shepherd One a twist of her hand.*]

BLIND DYKE: THERE!

SHEPHERD ONE [*screams with pain*]: ANYTHING BUT DAT! I WILL LEAD YOU TO WHERE I SAW THE VULTURE KING—OR GOD—OR WHATEVER HE IS!
[*Aside*] Little does she know that my buddy Shepherd Two will soon catch up with us. We will croak the Blind Dyke together and sell her to the glue factory. Heh-heh.
O.K. you have persuaded me Blind Dyke. I will do it.

BLIND DYKE: So you won't give me the slip I will tie you to me with this rope.

SHEPHERD ONE: JUST AS YOU SAY, BLIND DYKE.
[*Aside*] All da better so's I can slow you down till me buddy gets here with the ax.

BLIND DYKE: GET ME TO THE VULTURE KING PRONTO OR I'LL BEAT THE STUFFING OUT OF YOU!

SHEPHERD ONE: ANYTING YOU SAY, MISS.
[*Aside*] Heh-heh.

[*The Blind Dyke and Shepherd One exit the stage tied together with rope.*]

VOICE OF THE BLIND DYKE: GORFETTA-A-A-A-A-A. . . I COME TO AVENGE YOU!

[*Pause. The stage is empty. Shepherd Two runs onto the stage puffing.*]

SHEPHERD TWO: HEY, WHERE'S MY OLD BUDDY? Puff. Puff. [*He looks around.*] Look, dere's his footprints.

And some huge footprints beside his. It's a good ting I got me ax.

[*Shepherd Two runs off stage following the footprints.*]

[*Pause. The stage is empty. TV One and TV Two run on stage.*]

TV ONE: Oh, sirrahs, sirrah shepherds! Where are you?

TV TWO: They're really so neat!

TV ONE AND TV TWO: Whether there's weather or not. [*They embrace and kiss.*] SMACK! SMACK!

[*The TVs pause looking in each other's eyes.*]

TV ONE [*looks down*]: Look! Footprints.

TV TWO: Yes! Wow! Footprints!

[*The TVs run off stage following the footprints.*]

TV ONE AND TV TWO: Hey wait! Wait for us! Wait shepherds, wait for us! It's us, TV One and TV Two.

[*Black*]

Scene Nine

[*A roadside at the foot of the mountains. A sign pointing off stage says—Thebes. Pause. Enter the Giant Penguin with backpack and staff. He sings and is accompanied by the Chorus of Naked Stars. The music is wander-music.*]

GIANT PENGUIN:
[*Song*]
JOY, JOY, JOY SUBLIME—
FEEL THE NEARING OF TIME.
JOY, JOY, JOY WITHOUT CRIME—
SENSE THE PASSING OF SPACE.
No longer do we need to pantomime
what our being does.
We can smile with our bodies
and garden with our face.
JOY, JOY, JOY SUBLIME—NEARING OF TIME.
JOY WITHOUT CRIME—PASSING OF SPACE.

CHORUS:
JOY, JOY, JOY SUBLIME—NEARING OF TIME.
JOY WITHOUT CRIME—PASSING OF SPACE.
[*The Chorus leader steps forward*:]
Speak, speak, oh Giant Penguin. Pray
tell us quick. Is today the day?

GIANT PENGUIN [*stepping front*]: Ahem. . . Yes, I accept
that you call me "Giant Penguin." [*Pause*] I have willingly
assumed this guise as clothing to be worn in my search for
the other particles of The Shitfer. For above all things you
must remember. . .

[*Short song*]
For above all things you must remember
that I the Giant Penguin am a particle of The Shitfer.
I the Giant Penguin am a particle of The Shitfer
—above all things that is what you must remember.

CHORUS:
Yes, yes, we understand.
Oh particle of The Shitfer, Giant Penguin, pray
tell us quick. Is today the day?

59

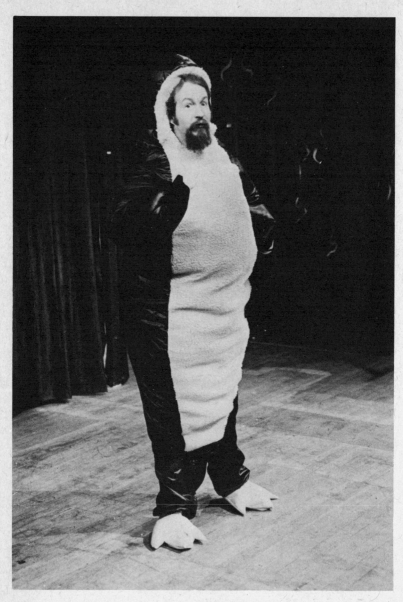

The Giant Penguin.

[*The Chorus does high-kicks and throws
handfuls of glitter.*]

Yes? Yes? Yes?
Is today the day?
Answer us quickly—yea or nay!

GIANT PENGUIN: Before the sqwunch of Time and Space,
before the abyss was Abyssinia. . . [*Pause*] Before the giant
hairy elephant sat on Mert and Gert. . . [*Pause*] In the olden
times that precede these days of myth. [*Pause*] When things
were real. [*Pause*] When the snooty-rootian movements still
jiggled in all the bumps that matter is made up of. . .
Then. . . [*Pause*] Then The Shitfer was one. Then The
Shitfer was just one thing. Everything else was well, and
whole, and happy, and the olive grew, and the duck fell
down with a heart attack at the foot of the hunter.

CHORUS:
JOY—JOY SUBLIME—NEARING OF TIME!
JOY—JOY WITHOUT CRIME—PASSING OF SPACE!
Is today the day?
Yea or nay?

GIANT PENGUIN: Ahem. . . [*Pause, slowly*] As a Particle
of The Shitfer my answer is not an easy thing. As a giant
penguin it would be simpler. Since Pre-Mythic meaning lies
in being a piece of The Shitfer I will answer you in that
voice of ancient meaningness of beingness that lies in matter.
My words will not flatter your scattered stellar ears.

CHORUS [*apprehensively*]: His words will not flatter our
scattered stellar ears?

GIANT PENGUIN: Ahem. . . [*Pause*] There isn't no thing
that happens away from the fact that it moves. If something

61

jiggles then it IS. If it wiggles then it has got BEING by the tail and it can bite and it can smile.

CHORUS:
If something jiggles then it IS. . .
If it wiggles it has got *being* by the tail
and it can bite
and it can smile. . . ?

GIANT PENGUIN: Ahem. . . [*Pause*] Yes, if it does not do anything and it just dreams that it is—even if it dreams that it is flying around. . .

CHORUS: Even if it dreams that it is flying around. . . ?

GIANT PENGUIN: Yep. . . Even if it dreams it is flying around then it is not anything! Not if it is dreaming. Nope! It is not a thing if it is dreaming. Because if something, whether it is alive or dead, is going to BE then it's got to BE and it can't BE dreaming. Can't be part of a myth— if you see what I mean.

CHORUS: It can't be part of a myth if you see what he means!

GIANT PENGUIN: IT HAS GOT TO BE REAL LIKE THE SHITFER—OR IT DON'T MEAN BEANS!

CHORUS:
IT HAS GOT TO BE REAL AS THE SHITFER
OR IT DON'T MEAN BEANS!
None of that myth and none of that guff
is half as good as touchable stuff!

GIANT PENGUIN: BECAUSE IT IS ALCHEMICAL AND MYSTIC!

CHORUS: YEAH, YEAH, THE TOUCHABLE STUFF IS ALCHEMICAL AND MYSTIC!

GIANT PENGUIN: THEREFORE. . . [*Pause*] THERE-FORE I CAN'T TELL YOU WHAT IS HAPPENING TILL IT IS GOING ON. . .

CHORUS: THEREFORE HE CAN'T TELL US WHAT IS HAPPENING TILL IT IS GOING ON.

GIANT PENGUIN: Once it is going on—when it has really started to happen—then it has got relationship to The Shitfer! Even when The Shitfer is splintered The Shitfer is a field. Like a lodestone—it draws itself together.

CHORUS:
Everything that's real has got
a relationship to The Shitfer.
The Shitfer, when it is splintered,
sets up a field
like a lodestone
to draw itself together. . .

GIANT PENGUIN: Ahem. . . [*Pause*] So I stand here a Pre-Mythic particle of The Shitferian Oneness. I know that my existence is an action that draws all things together. . . [*French horns sound in the distance.*] As long as there is a purple hero, reality will last!

CHORUS: A purple hero?

[*French horns sound in distance.*]

GIANT PENGUIN: Yes. Ahem. . . [*Pause*] There's got to be a purple hero to keep The Shitfer one—even when The Shitfer is sailing toward Arcturus.

The dance and song of the Giant Penguin and the
chorus of Naked Stars.

CHORUS:
A PURPLE HERO?
A PURPLE HERO—WHO COULD THAT BE?
[*Pantomiming a search*]
Would we find him in a tidepool?
Would we find him in a tree?

GIANT PENGUIN: The purple hero is a catalyst. Without him even The Mighty Shitfer could fall apart and crumble.

CHORUS AND GIANT PENGUIN:
[*Song*]
WITHOUT THE PURPLE HERO
EVEN THE MIGHTY SHITFER
COULD FALL APART AND CRUMBLE.
Yet it is possible he's ignorant
and doesn't give a tumble
to the fact that he must act with tact. . .
[*Pause*]
To pull The Shitfer back together.
To pull The Shitfer back together.

[*The Blind Dyke staggers onto the stage bound to the Shepherd. She hurls herself about and gropes for landmarks.*]

CHORUS: Holy moly, what is that?

[*Chorus reply*]: I don't know but it is huge and blind and fat.

CHORUS: Golly sakes, there's two of them held together with a rope!

BLIND DYKE: WHERE'S HE AT? JUST POINT ME AT THAT VULTURE! I'LL TEAR HIM BEAK FROM

CLAW AND USE HIS TAIL BONE FOR A TOOTH-
PICK!

SHEPHERD ONE: O.K., I MADE THE DEAL WITH
YOU! NOW LEMME GO! I WANTA GET OUTTA DIS
SCAREY PLACE!

BLIND DYKE: POINT ME AT HIM!

[*Shepherd One points the Blind Dyke toward the Giant
Penguin.*]

HOW FAR IS HE?

SHEPHERD ONE: 'BOUT THREE AND A HALF
YARDS. . .

[*The Blind Dyke leaps on the Giant Penguin drawing
Shepherd One with her.*]

BLIND DYKE [*rage*]: YEEEEEEEEEEEEEEEE! DE-
VOURER OF GORFETTE!

[*The Giant Penguin is bowled over by the Blind Dyke
and by Shepherd One. The three make a writhing heap of
bodies on the stage—they clamber one on top of another.*]

GIANT PENGUIN: OOOOOOOOOOOOOF!

SHEPHERD ONE: YAHHHHGHH!

BLIND DYKE: GOTCHA! GOTCHA BY THE FEA-
THERS YOU ROTTEN DEMON BIRD!
BUT WAIT! [*Surprised and joyful*]
I FEEL STRANGE AND RADIANT!

SHEPHERD ONE: ME TOO!
JEEZ, I FEEL STRANGE AND RADIANT!

GIANT PENGUIN [*grasping the Blind Dyke*]: THIS IS AN-
OTHER PARTICLE OF THE SHITFER! [*His voice is
ecstatic.*] OH JOY!

CHORUS [*ecstatically*]: OHHHHH!

GIANT PENGUIN [*he grasps Shepherd One and cries out*]:
JOY! ESCTASY! HERE IS ANOTHER PARTICLE OF
THE SHITFER!

SHEPHERD ONE: JEEZ. I FEEL NEAT! Wow!

CHORUS [*ecstatically*]: OHHHHHHHHHH!
Praise, praise to the gods for now on this day there are
three particles of The Shitfer. Let us begin a solemn dance
of thanksgiving.
[*Bells of thanksgiving begin in the distance.*]

CHORUS [*beginning the dance*]: JOY, JOY THAT THERE
ARE THREE PARTICLES OF THE SHITFER: THE
BLIND DYKE, SHEPHERD ONE, AND THE GIANT
PENGUIN ALL JOINED TOGETHER. . . IEEEE! OH!
ALOHA-IEEE!

[*Shepherd Two runs on stage brandishing his ax. He runs
right at the Blind Dyke and the Giant Penguin, who are
part of the ecstatic tableau with Shepherd One.*]

SHEPHERD TWO: O.K., YOU MUDDERS! LEAVE GO
OF MY BUDDY! IT IS DE MARBLE ORCHARD FOR
YOU! [*He brings down the ax at the Giant Penguin. The
Blind Dyke grasps the ax and stays it in midair.*]
OH HAPPINESS. WHAT IS DIS JOYFUL FEELING

OF RADIANCE? SURELY I IS NOT ME BUT I AM
SOMETHING MORE. HEY, I FEELS LIKE I BATHED
IN A STEAMY HOLE AND HAD SATIN SHEETS—
OR LIKE A LITTLE RIVER FILLED WIT MINNOWS!
WOW!

GIANT PENGUIN [*with solemn humming by the Chorus*]:
IT IS A FOURTH PARTICLE OF THE SHITFER!

[*Bells of thanksgiving*]

CHORUS: OHHHHHHH! JOY, JOY THAT THERE
ARE FOUR PARTICLES OF THE SHITFER: THE
BLIND DYKE, SHEPHERD ONE, THE GIANT PEN-
GUIN, AND SHEPHERD TWO—ALL JOINED TO-
GETHER. . . IEEE! OH! ALOHA-IEEE! Praise, praise
this blessing with our solemn dance!

[*Mert and Gert run in from opposite sides of the stage
and collide in front of the tableau. They cry out
"WOOOOOOOOOOOO. . ." as they run.*]

MERT [*colliding and falling over*]: Hey, Gert, it is you!

GERT: Mert!

MERT: Yes!

GERT: Where are we? I feel so strange!
Why it is almost as if we and The Shitfer was back together.

CHORUS: ALOHA-IEEE! ALOHA-IEEE! JOY! HYM-
NUS! IEEE!

GERT: Hey, look Mert, the snakes is dropping out of my

68

Gert and Mert and the almost reunited Shitfer.

hair! Yeah and the black ribbons is dropping from our limbs! Look, the snakes are dropping out of your hair too!

MERT: I feel good, Gert, but strange too! I feel better than I have since we died. Who is this Chorus though? And where are we? Look! Look!

[*Mert and Gert stagger against The Four Particles of the Shitfer that stand in noble tableau.*]

BLIND DYKE [*grasping Gert*]: MOTHER!

SHEPHERD ONE [*grasping Mert*]: FADDER!

SHEPHERD TWO AND GIANT PENGUIN [*together*]: MOTHER AND FATHER—REUNITED WITH THE SHITFER!

CHORUS: ALOHA-IEEE! MOTHER AND FATHER ARE REUNITED WITH THE SHITFER! PARTICLES AND PARENTS JOINING TOGETHER. . . HAPPINESS! ALOHA-IEEE!

GERT: RADIANCE! OH JOY!

MERT: AT LAST! I REALLY FEEL NEAT! WOW! WOW!

[*Mert and Gert become part of The Tableau of the Shitfer.*]

[*The Tableau of the Shifter is a complex body-sculpture of beings in various united postures of ecstasy and transfiguration.*]

[*Gorf flies in blowing his horn: "TAR-AHHHHHHHH! TAH-REEEEEEEEEEEEH. . ."*]

GORF [*pausing in mid-air*]: Holy gee! It is many particles of The Shitfer—they are beings that previously I knew in their separateness and now they join together! Hmmmm. . . I must think about this. [*He blows his horn.*]

CHORUS [*seeing Gorf*]: GORF, GORF, YOU'VE DONE IT AGAIN!
GORF, GORF YOU'RE EVERYBODY'S FRIEND!
YOU'RE THE PURPLE HERO!

VOICE: THREE CHEERS FOR GORF!

CHORUS: HURRAH. . .

[*TV One and TV Two rush in and add to the cheers. TV One and TV Two are carrying the dead sheep between them.*]

TV ONE: Wait, oh Shepherd, we have thy lost sheep.

TV TWO: Yes, here it is and it is really neat. [*The TVs struggle across the stage with the dead sheep.*]

TV ONE [*pointing*]: Hey, that is neat!

TV TWO: Yes, it is really neat. That is The Tableau of the Almost Completed Shitfer!

CHORUS: HYMNUS! ALOHA-IEEE! [*Chimes of thanksgiving. Madrigals of hums.*]

[*The Naked Girl with Fairy Wings darts on stage and takes the dead sheep from the TVs as if it were weightless.*]

NAKED GIRL: Here, I'll take that.

[The Naked Girl darts to The Tableau of the Shitfer and climbs part way up the body-sculpture, holding the dead sheep above her head.]

CHORUS *[transported]*: HYMNUS! HYMNUS! ALOHA-AIEEEEEE!

[Gorf flies around blowing his horn.]

GIANT PENGUIN *[full profundity]*: Ahem. . . *[Pause]* With the addition of the Naked Girl with Fairy Wings and the dead sheep all particles of The Shitfer are hereby declared united. . .

CHORUS: ALL OF THE PARTICLES OF THE SHITFER ARE DECLARED UNITED!

GIANT PENGUIN: PRAISE TO THE GODS!

CHORUS: Praise! PRAISE!

GIANT PENGUIN: SOON THERE WILL BE THE TRANS-MOGRIFICATION OF THE DIMENSIONS!

CHORUS: THERE WILL BE THE TRANSMOGRIFICA-TION OF THE DIMENSIONS!

GIANT PENGUIN: FIRST WILL COME THE UN-SQWUNCHING TOGETHER OF TIME AND SPACE.

CHORUS: THE UN-SQWUNCHING TOGETHER OF TIME AND SPACE!

GIANT PENGUIN: IT WILL COME IN THE FORM OF A GIANT BUMP!

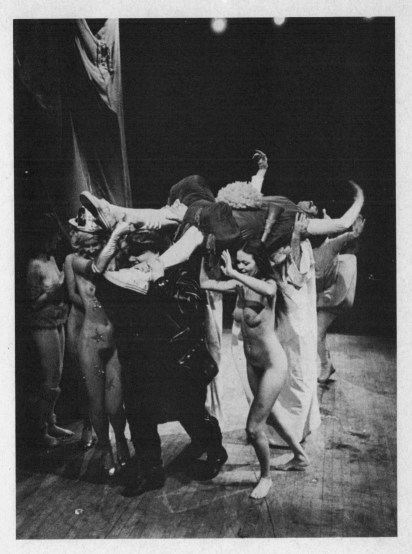

Gorf carried away with the Dance of Thanks Giving.

CHORUS: GIANT BUMP!

[*There is the huge amplified sound of the Giant Bump.*]

GIANT BUMP: *BUMP!!!!*

[*There are many pink smoke effects, light effects, and waterfalls, and light projections. The Tableau of the Shitfer writhes ecstatically.*]

CHORUS: OHH! AHH! IT IS THE BUMP! IT IS THE MOMENT OF TRANSMOGRIFICATION!

GIANT PENGUIN: WITH THE REUNITING OF THE SHITFER COMES THE FINISH OF THE AGE OF MYTH.

CHORUS: DOWN WITH THE AGE OF MYTH! HURRAH FOR REALITY!

[*A Giant Hairy Elephant sits down on the stage covering the whole Tableau of the Shitfer with a huge woolly tarpaulin. The tarpaulin remains and covers The Tableau of the Shitfer, which jiggles and trembles beneath the tarpaulin.*]

[*Gorf flies about blowing his horn. There are flickerings of light. Rainbows and thunderstorms.*]

CHORUS: THE GIANT HAIRY ELEPHANT SAT ON THE TABLEAU OF THE UNITED SHITFER AT THE PRECISE MOMENT OF THE UN-SQWUNCHING OF TIME AND SPACE FOLLOWING THE GIANT BUMP!

VOICE OF THE GIANT PENGUIN [*from under the woolly tarpaulin*]: BY GOLLY, DON'T WORRY—ALL IS AS IT SHOULD BE!

VOICE OF THE BLIND DYKE: THIS IS DESTINY!

VOICE OF SHEPHERD ONE: IT IS THE WILL OF THE KNOWING ONES!

VOICE OF THE NAKED GIRL: Delight! Delight unending!

VOICE OF THE DEAD SHEEP: BAAaa-a-a-a. . . Baa-a-a. . .

VOICE OF SHEPHERD TWO: Heaven! HEAVEN!

VOICE OF MERT: I always told you it would be like this, Gert! This is better than DEEtroit!

VOICE OF GERT: You always did say that Mert! At last we are one with The Shitfer!

[*The huge shape of the United Shitfer begins to dance under the tarpaulin—it is more than ten feet tall.*]

CHORUS [*transported, dancing all around the tarpaulin of The Shitfer*]: JOY! JOY! ALOHA-IEEE! REALITY! REALITY; EVERYTHING REAL AGAIN; HYMNUS! PERFECT PERFECTION! [*The Chorus chants and hums. Gorf flies over blowing his horn softly.*]

TV ONE AND TV TWO: Whether there's weather or not! SMACK! SMACK!

TV ONE: Hey Gorf, the prophesy said, "Gorf of all shall bring the godlike to a glowing gleam."

TV TWO: Sure! We believe in you, Gorf, but remember it said: "Gorf of all shall bring the godlike to a glowing gleam." So where is the glowing gleam, Gorf?

75

TV ONE: Yes, where is the glowing gleam? We do not understand.

[*As The Shitfer dances, staffs are pushed through the woolly tarpaulin, and on the end of the staffs are old-fashioned lanterns and they glow in the dimming stage light and make patterns in the air as The Shitfer wobbles and dances.*]

CHORUS [*in pure ecstasy*]: THE GODLIKE IS BROUGHT TO A GLOWING GLEAM! THE GODLIKE IS BROUGHT TO A GLOWING GLEAM! ALOHA-IEEE! HYMNUS! JOY! JOY! [*Etc. They dance around The Shitfer.*]

TV ONE AND TV TWO: SMACK! SMACK!

[*Gorf flies around blowing his horn.*]

[*Waterfall effects. Rainbows. Projections. Movies. Smoke. Voices sighing in ecstasy.*]

CHORUS:
GORF, GORF, YOU'VE DONE IT AGAIN!
GORF, GORF, YOU'RE EVERYBODY'S FRIEND!
YOU'RE THE PURPLE HERO!

VOICE: THREE CHEERS FOR GORF!

VOICE: YES, THREE CHEERS FOR GORF!

CHORUS: HURRAH! HURRAH! HURRAH!

[*Gorf flies around blowing his horn while The Shitfer dances with the lanterns and the Chorus dances around The Shitfer.*]

Ecstatic song of the wholly completed Shitfer.

GORF: WOW! THIS IS NEAT!

EVERYBODY:
[*Song and dance*]
PUT YOUR FINGERS ON A STAR
or you won't get very far
but no matter who you are
YOU
GOTTA
LEARN
to take good care of yourself!
All the rip-offs and all the pelf
certainly can't be good for your health!

You're a little baby sweet,
when you see that everything is neat—
'cause
you
know
you gotta play fair.

All the universe is just a curl in your hair—
and baby bears are sleeping in caves—
and surely you know
you're nobody's slave.

Put your fingers on a star
and recall that you're brave.
Everybody
you ever wanted to know
is right here
and you're nobody's slave!

Don't be afraid to take a little poke
'cause you know that reality is a joke.
Nothing can be sacred

or scared
unless it's part of the stairs!
And you know that everything
—every turtle dove, mastodon, and guitar—
are
a
part
of
your
affairs.
All the rip-offs and the pelf
certainly can't be good for your health!

PUT YOUR FINGERS ON A STAR. . . !

[*Everyone dances. Waterfall effects, dry ice, projections,
slides, films, lanterns, flashlights; Chorus throws glitter
and does high-kicks. Gorf flies around blowing his horn.
The TVs kiss. The Shitfer dances and sways. Chimes of
thanksgiving. . . Etc.*]

FINIS